Animal Disguises

Animal Disguises

by Aileen Fisher

designed and illustrated by Tim and Greg Hildebrandt

lettering by Paul Taylor

...to Flossy

We looked at a twig,
but it wasn't a twig.
It wasn't a twig at all.

6

It looked twiggy thin, with a rough sort of skin, and clung to a branch near the wall.

It was a caterpillar.

We
looked
at a
stone
where
the
meadow
was mown,
a
stone
colored
brownish
and
gray.

But
it
Wasn't
a stone.

When a pebble was thrown, it suddenly bounded a-w-a-y.

It was a rabbit.

We looked at some bark
quite ragged and dark

and mottled
and streaky and small,

It pretended to be a part of the tree, but it actually wasn't a

It was a moth.

We looked
through
a door
of the
woods
at
the
floor
of sun-speckled leaves all around.

Then W-W-W-whush!!!

with a start
the "leaves" burst a-p-a-r-t
like a bombshell
concealed
on the ground.

Seven bobwhites!

We looked at some reeds where a water bird breeds.

but saw nothing birdlike at all,

till we made out a bill, tilting steeply uphill, and a neck stretching reedlike and tall.

It was a bittern.

We looked at a leaf that wasn't a leaf
although it was leaf-colored green
and shaped like a leaf
and veined like a leaf

to fit in the summery scene.

It was a katydid.

Oh, an animal's clothes,

or his shape,

or his pose,

if the animal's tiny or

tall,

or trick you to think

he's something he isn't at all.

Tail Twisters Filling the Bill Sleepy Heads Going Places Animal Jackets Tail Twisters Robin to the Fawn Animal Houses Now That Days Are Colder No Accounting For Tastes Animal Jackets Tail Twisters Filling the Bill Sleepy Heads Going Places Animal "You Don't Look Like Your Mother," Said the Robin to the Fawn Animal Disguises "You Don't Look Like Your Mother," Said the Robin